Sleeping is Boring!

Ida Susan,

Dream Big Little Angel

Brianna Snel

Sleeping is Boring!

Written by Brianna Snel

StarLight Books

Sleeping Is Boring!

ISBN Number 979-8-9901875-1-1
LCCN Number 2024917043

StarLight Books Publishing
www.starlightbooks.net

Illustrator Esther Rai
Editor Blair Thornburgh & StarLight Books

Dedication

This book is dedicated to my five year old daughter, Isla. Each night while tucking her into bed she would often tell us that bedtime was boring, sleeping is boring. Her mind was in so many other places, thinking of all the things she could be doing instead. Her imagination and creativity inspired me to show what so many little kids are thinking about when they are told they need to go to bed.

I'd also like to dedicate my first book to my mom, Kim. For years she has told me that I should and could write a book. After starting and stopping a few times, I finally listened to her and my heart, and put my thoughts onto the page.

Thank you mom for your constant love and support.

"I don't want to go to bed!" Isla announced to her mom as she was putting on her favorite purple pajamas with the rainbow stars on them.

“Bedtime is boring! Sleeping is boring!”
She roughly yanked the blankets down and climbed into her bed with a giant frown on her face and a pleading look in her eyes.

"Okay," her mother said.
"If sleeping is SO boring, what would you do instead?"

Grinning ear to ear, Isla sat up in her bed.

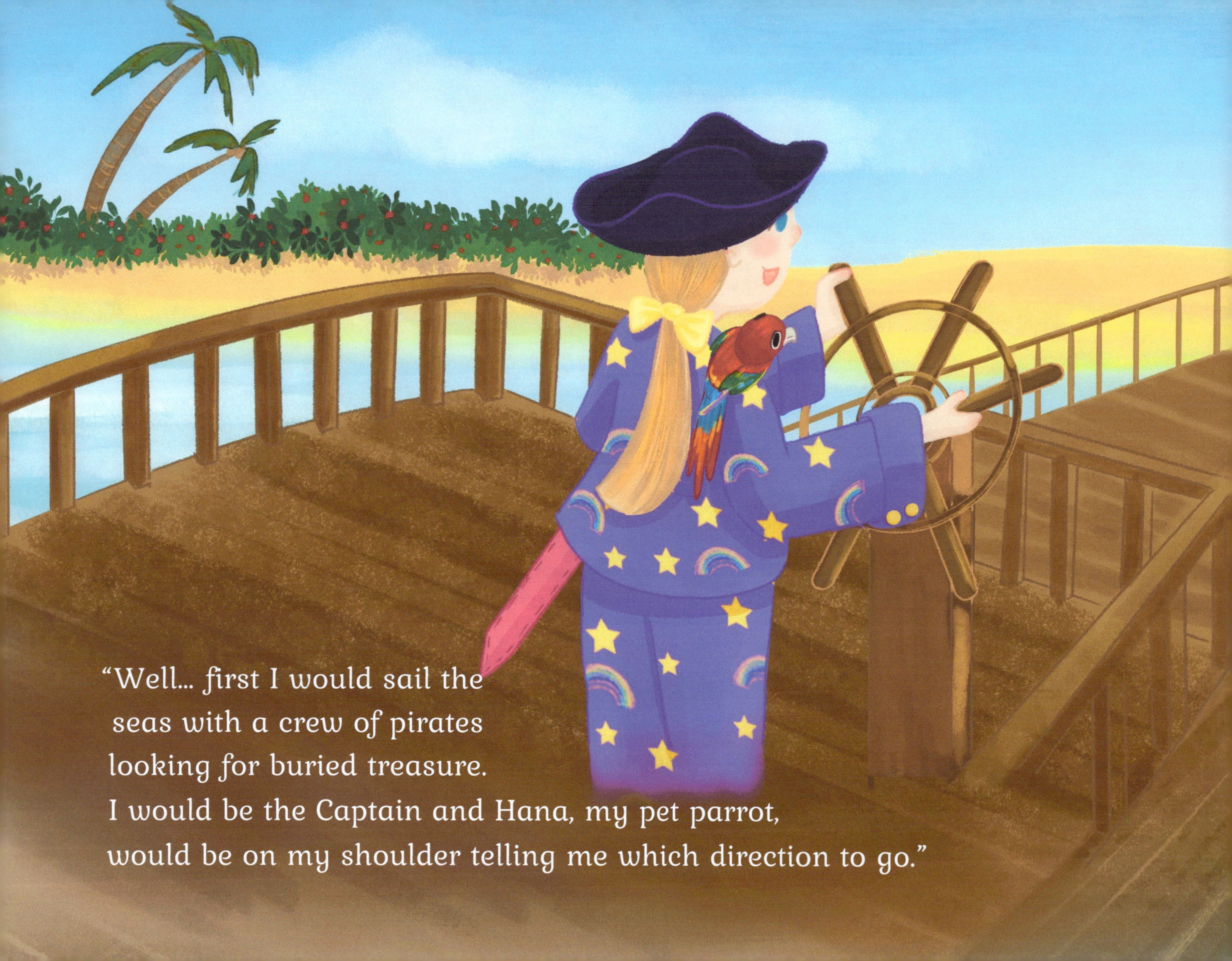

"Well… first I would sail the
seas with a crew of pirates
looking for buried treasure.
I would be the Captain and Hana, my pet parrot,
would be on my shoulder telling me which direction to go."

Isla stood up on her bed with her hand over her eyes pretending like she was searching. Once we got the treasure, we would bring it home and share it with our friends and family. There would be a big old brown trunk with more gold coins than you could count, and jewels that sparkled in every color of the rainbow."

"Oh, that would be very nice of you pirates to share your treasure." Isla's mother sounded surprised as she turned on Isla's nightlight. Then she bent over to pick up Isla's crumpled pile of clothes that were lying on the floor. She tossed them into the hamper in the closet and shut the door.

“We are the nice pirates, mom!” Isla groaned.
How did her mother not already know that? Also, because she was still making her go to bed despite her protests.

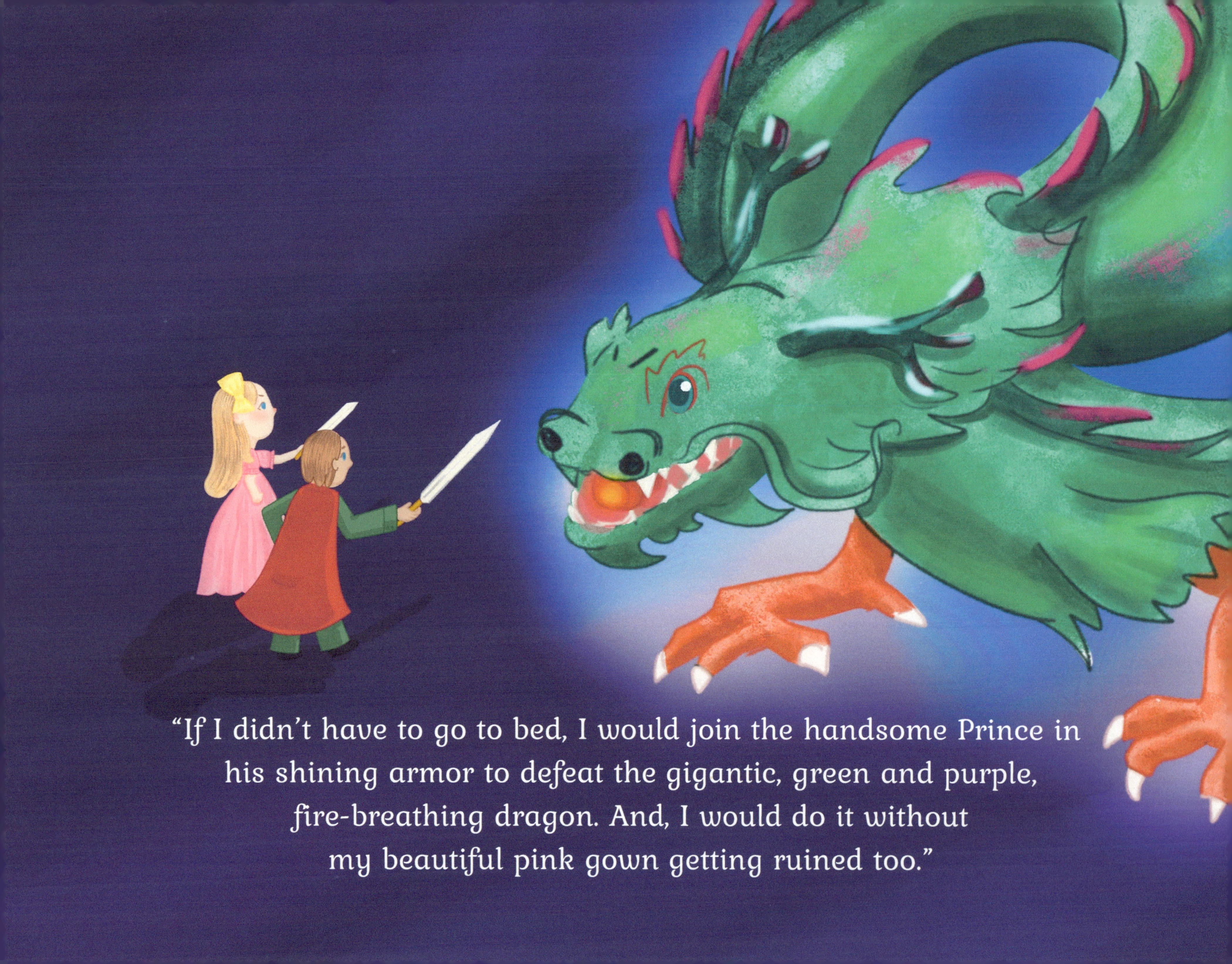

"If I didn't have to go to bed, I would join the handsome Prince in
his shining armor to defeat the gigantic, green and purple,
fire-breathing dragon. And, I would do it without
my beautiful pink gown getting ruined too."

Isla jumped off her bed and began twirling in circles. "After, we would dance and sing with all the people in the kingdom to celebrate," she announced triumphantly.

“That sounds like a wonderful adventure,” Isla’s mother replied. She pointed toward the bathroom to remind Isla that she still needed to brush her teeth.

“If I didn’t have to go to bed, I could ride my pet unicorn on all the rainbows. Sleeping is boring, but that would definitely NOT be boring!”

With a mouth full of toothpaste Isla exclaimed,
"Or I could become a mermaid and swim with the other
mermaids and explore the ocean floor."

Isla wiped her face and walked back into her bedroom. "The mermaids and I would make friends with all the sea creatures, especially whales and giant sea turtles. We could string some dazzling pearls and shells to make fancy necklaces to wear."

“Sleeping is so boring. You can’t see new places in a hot air balloon if you are in bed,” Isla sighed. Her mother replaced the books on the floor back into the bookshelf, as Isla picked out her pink dress and rainbow sneakers to wear to school the next day.

Smiling at her very imaginative daughter, her mother waited for Isla to climb back into bed. Then she laid her rainbow unicorn blanket on top of her, tucking her in.

Snuggled in her bed, Isla said, “If I didn’t have to go to bed,
I could be climbing the tallest mountain. Once I got to the top,
I could have a camp out underneath a million sparkly stars.”

“Wouldn’t you go to bed then?” Her mother sat down next to her on the bed. “Surely you would be exhausted after that!”

"Nope," Isla said more quietly as a yawn slipped out.
She grabbed her golden retriever stuffy, Roscoe,
and rolled onto her side to *face* her mother.

"Roscoe and I could be blasting off into space
to see the moon and sun, and all the planets in our solar system."
Isla kissed the stuffy and hugged him tightly to her chest.

"It sounds like you just have no time for sleep,"
said Isla's mother. "Do you, Isla?"

But Isla's eyes were closed and her chest was
rising and falling ever so gently.

“Goodnight my beautifully imaginative girl,” Isla’s mother whispered.
“I cannot wait to hear what journey you went on tonight.”

Her mother kissed her soft rosy cheek and brushed the hair out of her eyes. She walked to the door and turned around. Right before she turned out the light, she could see a smile form on Isla's face.

Whatever dream she was in, she was happy.
Maybe sleep wasn't so boring after all.

The End

About The Author

Brianna Snel is a fourth grade teacher who loves teaching language arts. Her love of reading and all things books has been a constant her whole life. After getting her Masters in Reading, she realized that she wanted to revisit her dream of writing children's books.

She lives at the Jersey Shore with her loving husband, three amazing children, and their loyal Golden Retriever. It was while putting her kids to bed each night that she fell back in love with the world of picture books and the magical experiences they bring you. Aside from reading, she enjoys runs to and along the beach and doing arts and crafts.

She is excited to bring all of her ideas, many inspired by her family, to life in her children's books.

www.authorbriannasnel.com

Printed in the USA
CPSIA information can be obtained
at www.ICGtesting.com
JSHW041908011024
70761JS00004B/6